TWISTAPLOT™

5

You're starring on TV tonight. But is it a comedy... or a horror show?

THE SINISTER STUDIOS OF KESP-TV

Louise Munro Foley

ILLUSTRATIONS BY DAVID FEBLAND

SCHOLASTIC INC.
New York Toronto London Auckland Sydney Tokyo

For my friend Bessie Heller—
86 years, a star

ISBN 0-590-32827-1

Copyright © 1983 by Louise Munro Foley. All rights reserved. Published by Scholastic Inc.

12 11 10 9 8 7 6 5 4 3 2   4 5 6 7/8

BEWARE!!!
DO NOT READ THIS BOOK FROM BEGINNING TO END

You are about to begin the television career you have always dreamed about. But before you tune in to this glamorous world of adventure, be warned: KESP-TV may be more than you bargained for.

As soon as you turn these pages, you will discover that television is more than bright lights, fame, and free limousines. Danger, kidnappings, espionage are all part of the programs on KESP-TV. Turn the wrong page — or turn on the wrong monitor — and you could find yourself in the hands of enemy agents. Get in front of that camera, and your television career could be very short!

What happens depends on you. If you get into trouble, turn back and choose a different way out. If you like being a Star, keep going!

So tune in and find out what the exciting world of television is all about.

You're on the air!

Now turn to PAGE 2.

2

"The real world of work is not what you imagine. You don't just go to your job every day and collect your money every two weeks . . ."

Mrs. Downing's voice drones on.

Originally, you thought the Career Counseling class would be fun, but all it's been is tests, tests, and Mrs. Downing.

"The aptitude scores are back, and from the results I have selected four students to take part in a work-study program."

This class is dumb, you write on a corner of your math homework. You tear off the note and pass it to Hank in the next aisle.

"Four employers have each agreed to take one student as part of the project," Mrs. Downing continues.

You glance up with a little more interest. That sounds like a chance to skip school — with permission! You look over at Hank.

Skip on over to PAGE 3.

Hank is listening to Mrs. Downing with more interest, too.

"The employers are: Drucker's Plumbing, The Mustard Seed Restaurant, Martell's Department Store, and . . . KESP-TV."

You sit bolt upright. KESP-TV! You'd give your right arm to work there! You can just picture yourself — talking with celebrities, doing a commercial, starring in your own show!

Mrs. Downing interrupts your daydream. "Based on the aptitude tests, the students I have chosen are: Mary Smurdock, Drucker's Plumbing; Hank Blackwell, The Mustard Seed Restaurant; Nina Nochales, Martell's Department Store; and for KESP-TV —"

You don't believe it! Did she really call your name? She sure did!

"Since we can't take time from the school schedule for this project, workdays have been scheduled during the spring break."

Part of you groans a little. But just a little. You're willing to give up part of spring break if it means a job in television.

You're going to be a Star!

Shoot over to PAGE 4, Star!

The Saturday morning you report for work is oddly stormy. Black clouds hang over everything, even though the weather report for today said there would be clear, sunny weather. The air is as suffocating as a blanket.

You walk into the brightly lit lobby of KESP-TV, expecting to see newscasters, camera people, and engineers running around. Strange. Except for the oversized photos of the broadcast crew lining the stark white walls, the lobby is deserted. The TV monitors on the walls are black.

This looks more like an empty studio set than the bustling television station you imagined. Why isn't there anyone here?

Lost in thought, you trip over the lace of one of your new jogging shoes and sit down at the desk to retie it. That's when you see the memo.

ATTENTION, KESP PERSONNEL:
Unable to contact Career Counseling student. Too late to cancel or reschedule.

You frown indignantly. *So they tried to cancel you out! Well, tough! You're here, and you're not leaving!*

Behind the desk is a door marked AUTHORIZED PERSONNEL ONLY.

If you decide that you're authorized, turn to PAGE 7.

If you think you should wait in the lobby, turn to PAGE 9.

You walk to the file cabinet with a sheaf of papers from the file basket, still puzzling over Betsy's note.

You check your watch. 12:40. Time is crawling.

You mechanically stuff papers into file folders and periodically glance at the monitors. You wish you knew more about weather systems. You also wish you knew if Betsy were coming back.

12:50. You just know she is not coming back.

The Bishop weather station monitor sits, gray and dull, like an overcast day. You no longer have any urge to turn it on. Fleetingly, you wonder what happens to a phased-out weather station.

12:55. You reread Betsy's note. You must call Col. Corkley now.

You grab the phone and ask the operator to connect you with Col. Corkley at the Pentagon.

Connect up with PAGE 58.

You push open the door and enter a long, wide hall. On the floor, four trails of colored footprints lead to various doors: green prints to a green door; yellow prints to a yellow door; red to what must be the studio, because a red light shines above the entrance. A trail of blue footprints disappears around the corner at the end of the hall.

What a dumb idea — it reminds you of your old first grade classroom.

> Green to the outside, red to the sink,
> Yellow to the cloakroom
> And blue to help you think!

The blue ones at school led to the library corner.

You know better than to barge into the studio. Better try one of the other doors.

Going for the green? Leaf over to PAGE 27.

Yellow? Be cautious ... and try PAGE 32.

Want to disappear around that corner? Take blue ... and turn to PAGE 28.

The astronaut you saw and Betsy's tornado conversation are still bothering you.

"About the astronaut you saw and about Betsy causing tornadoes . . ." says Paschal.

How did he know your thoughts?

"The phone call and the film clip were meant only to measure your curiosity quotient. It is quite high," he says.

Boy, was Mrs. Downing right! The world of work is not what you imagined . . .

"Yes," says Paschal. "Mrs. Downing was entirely correct."

"You're reading my mind!" you yell.

"It is my job," Paschal replies. "Do you think this place is called KESP-TV for nothing? Betsy and I have the sixth sense. We feel you have an even greater gift."

"Extra-sensory perception," you mutter. "KESP. I should have guessed."

Paschal nods. "It is a gift that can lead to great wealth. We are looking for a trainee. Mrs. Downing told us that you would be an apt student."

So she's in on this, too!

"Will you join us? The rewards are great."

"And if I don't?" you ask suspiciously.

"You are free to leave," he says.

Great wealth. Fortune. Is this a hoax?

Going to join Paschal and Betsy? Turn to PAGE 47.

Going to leave? Turn to PAGE 57.

You decide to wait a while. As you leaf through a magazine in the lobby, one of the phones rings. Once. Twice. Three times.

Grabbing the receiver, you say, "Good morning. KESP-TV."

"Betsy, please," a man says.

Your eye roams the wall of pictures and stops at a photograph of an attractive young woman standing at a weather board. Betsy is a well-known meteorologist.

"One moment, please." You push the hold button. You open the AUTHORIZED PERSONNEL door and find yourself facing the young woman from the photograph.

"For me?" she asks.

"Yes."

You sit down in an easy chair, pretending to read. But you can't help overhearing her agitated conversation.

"I said no tornadoes yet!" she snaps.

She slams down the receiver. "Are you the Career Counseling student?" she asks, annoyed that you showed up.

You nod.

"Come with me," she orders.

If you want to follow this whirlwind, turn to PAGE 36.

If you think you should have gone through the door earlier, you have learned a valuable lesson. Hindsight is better than foresight. Too bad, kid. Turn to PAGE 36.

Acting as if nothing is wrong, you get up from the desk and follow Betsy out of the office, down the long hall.

"No smart kid is going to upset my plan!" she says angrily. "The power to control the world is within my reach! You'll regret your meddling."

You know now that something sinister is definitely going on at KESP-TV. Betsy sounds more like some kind of enemy agent than a meteorologist. That astronaut you saw was no illusion, and Betsy's conversation about tornadoes wasn't an illusion either!

You're heading toward the lobby. If the police respond quickly, maybe they'll arrive in time to stop this madwoman!

You push open the door into the lobby. Coming through the double glass outer doors are two officers. Betsy turns and runs back down the hall.

"She's an enemy agent!" you yell. "Don't let her get away!"

One officer races after her. The other drapes his arm around your shoulders.

"You'll have to come to headquarters to give us a statement," he says, leading you to the patrol car.

Turn to PAGE 87.

You must get out of the control room to a phone, while Paschal is still on the air. You dash down the hall to an office and frantically dial the local police.

You blurt out your story about Paschal and Betsy and the museum curator and the jade and the combination to the vault.

The officer on the phone doesn't even have to reply to your eccentric story. *Thought waves must travel on phone lines,* you think, as you read his mind.

"Loony bin . . . weirdo . . . crackpot . . ." is coming through loud and clear.

"I am not!" you yell, as the dial tone hums in your ear.

You turn at the sound of a gentle, evil laugh behind you.

Betsy stands in the doorway. She is holding a small gun. "The combination, please," she says quietly.

Reluctantly, you hand over the paper.

"It is too bad," she says. "We thought you would make a fine accomplice."

"Don't think about it too much," you mutter, as she pulls the trigger. "Someone might read your mind."

THE END

He pushes a button, and a picture flips on the screen. Two men with stocking caps are inside what appears to be a bank.

"Now, Rocky and Clint are about to empty the First National vault," he says. "That alarm is on this lever. See? It's labeled. First National."

"I'm not stupid," you mutter.

He ignores your comment and continues. "Now, you push it up to set the alarm, and you pull it down to turn it off. Repeat after me. Up is on — down is off."

"Up is on — down is off," you repeat.

"Very good," he says. "Now pull it down."

"Pull it down?" you yell. "And be an accessory? Not me!"

"You don't want your cut of the take?" he asks.

"Cut?" you ask, puzzled.

His eyes narrow as he scrutinizes you carefully.

"Aren't you the parolee from the state pen?" he says suspiciously. "If you're not, then who are you? And how did you get in here?"

Going to tell him the truth? Turn to PAGE 15.

Going to lie? Turn to PAGE 45.

You follow Eban and Derk up a narrow flight of stairs and out to the lot where the KESP remote truck is parked. Eban gets into the driver's seat, and Derk motions stiffly for you to sit between them. You step over a puddle and climb in.

Go on to PAGE 14.

You notice that Eban's hands are folded in his lap. The wheel is turning with no help from the driver! The truck seems to be steered by remote control!

"What's going on here?" you yell at Derk.

That's when you see he is holding a small box. The box is labeled:

LASER BOX — 5 WATTS
TELETYPE NO. 4
DANGER

Derk's hands look strange. No wrinkles or hangnails. And Eban's are identical! They both move like machines, not human beings. You wonder if they *are* machines — robots! — controlled remotely by Larena.

"Your instructions are on Teletype No. 4," she said.

That explains the silent teletype. It's really her computer terminal to program Derk and Eban. And the Laser Box. Five watts sounds lethal! Is it also controlled by Teletype No. 4? You don't want to find out.

Think fast! Coming toward you is a police car. If you grab the wheel, maybe you can break the remote control pattern. Or maybe you can force the police car off the road!

If you decide to grab the wheel, force yourself to turn to PAGE 76.

If you choose to ride it out with the robots, turn to PAGE 88.

"I'm an escapee from Mrs. Downing's Career Counseling class," you mutter. "What's it to you?"

"You got spunk, kid," says Butch, nodding his approval. "I like that. You want in on the heist? We're shorthanded this week. Cops picked up three of my best."

"Best?" you repeat.

"Best board men!" Butch replies. "We're working two jobs this afternoon. Rocky and Clint at First National and Fingers and Joe over at Security Savings. Think you can handle the Security Savings job?"

"Up is on — down is off," you say, scowling. "I think I can handle it. What's my cut?"

"Ten percent of the take," says Butch. "And after three months you get a raise to fifteen percent — plus you get in on our group medical and pension plans."

"Deal," you say, sticking out your hand.

He rolls a desk chair up and motions you to sit down.

"Watch the clock," he instructs you. "Cut the alarm for Fingers and Joe at 2:08:25."

You nod as you watch your team at Security Savings on a second monitor, while Butch concentrates on the First National duo.

At exactly 2:08:25, you pull the lever down.

Continue on PAGE 33.

You smile at Paschal through the control room window and give him the thumbs up sign as Mr. Delman talks on about the jade collection.

Visions of a luxurious life dance through your head — Hawaii, Jordache jeans, a Porsche 924, crab's legs and steak dinners every night . . .

After the broadcast, Paschal and Betsy hurry you out of the control room to a car parked in the alley. It is dark. The streets are deserted.

When you arrive at the museum, Paschal opens a rear door with a passkey, and the three of you slip inside.

Pascal leads you straight to the vault that holds the jade. You hand him the paper on which the combination is written.

Your heart beats wildly as the metal door swings open to reveal the treasure . . . a treasure for you!

If you think you're going to get the jade, swing over to PAGE 80.

If you think you're going to get a surprise, turn to PAGE 92.

The general, still staring into space, has already started to respond to Hobart's loaded question.

You think of your little brother, Billy, and how he and his friends successfully interrupt your telephone conversations.

It just might work!

Strutting like a band major, you march toward the set, singing loudly.

"WHEN THE SAAAAAAINTS ..... GO MARCHING INNNNNNNN ..... "

The camera crew, puzzled, but enjoying your show, train their cameras on you.

"WHEN THE SAAAAAAINTS GO MARCHING INNNNNNNN ..... "

Hobart's face turns an angry red as he leans forward, straining to hear the general's words. The general appears bewildered by your actions but keeps on talking. *You must stop him!* Wheeling around, still singing, you march in front of him and grab the mike from his lapel, just as Hobart leaps up.

"Hold it!"

A voice rises above the clamor, and you swing around to see Larena and two policemen with their guns pointed at Hobart.

"Find out where he locked up the *real* Hobart," Larena orders the officers, as they lead Hobart Huckle away.

Then she turns to you.

And you turn to PAGE 53.

You look at the piece of paper that Betsy handed you. *Is it a joke?* This is no list of meteorological terms! The paper says:

I need your help. I am Lt. Col. Betsy Boggitt of the U.S. Air Force, working undercover at KESP-TV. The astronaut you saw is in a manned enemy satellite. A foreign power is trying to control our country's weather. If they succeed, this nation will be brought to its knees without any armed aggression. Their temporary base is a small cabin in Death Valley, where they will move me if they don't kill me first.

They already know who I am and what I am doing here. If I do not return by 1300 hours, call the Pentagon. Tell Col. Corkley where they have taken me. Do not talk to anyone here. One of the KESP staff is a spy. This room is bugged.

P.S. File the papers that are sitting in the file basket.

BB

1300 hours is military time for 1:00 PM! You check the overflowing file basket.

Going to sweat out the 30 minutes to see if Betsy returns? Turn to PAGE 6.
Going to go look for her? Go to PAGE 41.

You tighten your hold on the pepperoni stick. Slowly, you get to your feet. When you are almost standing, you fling the pepperoni past Larena to the center of the room.

Argenta leaps from Larena's shoulder in hot pursuit of the meat, knocking the commentator off balance.

You bolt from the newsroom into the hall, colliding head-on with a tall, handsome, dark-haired man with a beard.

"Hey!" he says, grabbing your arm.

"She's got a gun!" you gasp. "Larena has a gun!"

A frown flickers across his face, and his voice drops to a whisper. "So Luscious Larena's the one I've been sent to get." He lets go of your arm.

"Who are you?" you ask.

"Hobart Huckle, Secret Service," he whispers, flashing a badge. "But this week posing as Hobart Hansom, talk show announcer."

"Pleased to meet you," you say.

"No time for that," snaps Hobart. "Are you the Career Counseling kid?"

As you nod, you wonder how he knows you.

"Okay, kid. You're the only one around here I can trust. I'm deputizing you. Now listen closely and do exactly what I say."

Okay, kid, turn to PAGE 51.

You lower yourself into the hole, and Larena scrambles in after you. She pushes a button, and the teletype machine slips back over the opening. Angry voices overhead tell you that Hobart and his cohorts are in the newsroom.

"Give me your hand," Larena says.

Up ahead, you see a strange light moving in the darkness. As you are led along, you realize that the glow is coming from Argenta, who is leading Larena.

"Her coat is fluorescent," Larena explains.

The cat has stopped at a massive door, and Larena leans down to push a button at the base of the frame. The door slides open, revealing a brightly lit room full of people. Some of them look familiar. They are the people whose photos are in the lobby!

As you enter, a mighty cheer goes up.

"You did it!" yells a handsome, bearded, dark-haired man.

"It's Hobart!" you whisper.

"The real one!" Larena replies, throwing an arm over your shoulder.

"Who are these people?" you ask.

Who indeed? Introductions are made on PAGE 21.

"This," says Larena, "is the real Hobart Hansom, and these are members of the KESP-TV staff. They were locked down here on Friday night when the foreign impostors upstairs moved in. The impostors were going to use KESP's channel to broadcast classified material."

"That's why they tried to cancel my Career Counseling assignment," you say.

Larena nods. "Yes. They didn't want anyone around to interfere. When I found out they couldn't reach you, I knew I'd have to stop them — and look out for you, too."

"Humph," you say, somewhat miffed. "I can look out for myself."

"Of course," she says, smiling. "If you know what to look for."

"Why didn't they send an impostor for you?" you ask.

Hobart laughs. You turn. Standing beside him is another Larena.

"This is the real Larena," he explains. "And over there is the impostor Hobart Huckle brought."

In the corner sits a third Larena.

Hobart says, "We substituted our impostor for their impostor.

Real Larena—False Larena—Agent Larena. "Are you kidding?" you say.

If you understand, turn to PAGE 90.
If you don't understand, join the impostors, pretend you do, and turn to PAGE 90.

You stare up at The Box, then scan the alley. The city cleanup crew has done an excellent job. There is not a stray bottle, rock, or can anywhere in sight. Well, you know what your mother always says.

Necessity is the mother of invention.

Staying close to the wall, you bring your left foot up and untie one of your new white jogging shoes. Your fingers curl around the sole, and the sturdy rubber toeplate nestles firmly into your palm.

No warmups. No second chances.

You bring your arm back and release the shoe.

Arcing like a missile through the air, it sails gracefully into its target.

You hear a slight *whoosh* as The Box disintegrates, along with your shoe, and small fragments of metal and white rubber drop to the ground.

Hop over to PAGE 62.

"Come back into the weather studio!" Betsy's voice startles you. "Sorry I was so sharp. I didn't get much sleep last night."

"That's okay," you mumble, casting a quick glance at the astronaut's monitor. The screen is blank.

"Now, about the tornadoes," she says. "I wish I *could* turn them on and off! What I said on the phone was that there were no tornado patterns shaping up. You must have misunderstood."

"I must have," you murmur. But you know what you heard.

"What comes in on that screen?" you ask, pointing to the one where you saw the astronaut.

"That used to be the Bishop, California, weather station. Budget cuts phased it out in April. It's not transmitting anymore. . . . Here. Study this list of meteorological terms, while I take these updates to the studio."

Why is she lying to you?

She hands you a paper and pauses.

"Don't touch any of the monitors," she warns.

The door glides shut, and you turn and stare at the dead screen. Should you turn it on? Or study the list of terms?

If you decide to turn it on, turn to PAGE 46.

If you decide to study, retreat to PAGE 18.

"Who are you really?" you demand, getting out of the chair.

"You are strong-willed, aren't you?" says Larena, giving you an evil stare. "No one else has been able to resist the force of my electronic brain-scrambling chair!"

"My sister calls it dumb-stubborn," you mutter.

She acts as if she hasn't heard you. "It doesn't matter if I tell you why I'm here," she says. "You see, you'll never leave this room alive."

"So tell me," you say, as you inch closer to the control board.

"Hobart and I are agents from a tiny principality in the Near West. Our country has no huge military force. But we have devised a plan — a bloodless coup — by which we can bring your giant country to its knees!"

Her eyes glisten as she talks. She looks utterly mad.

"We have no powerful weapons or mighty fleets . . . but we have brains!"

As you listen, you are watching the flashing lights.

Interesting panel, you think. *Especially that bright orange lever on your left, marked MASTER.*

Going to succumb to temptation and grab the master lever? Turn to PAGE 86.

Or exercise patience and hear the rest of her crazy story? Turn to PAGE 39.

You creep up so quietly that the man at the control board doesn't hear you. As you get closer, you notice that there are labels above the switches on the control panel. FIRST NATIONAL BANK, SECURITY SAVINGS, TITLE TRUST COMPANY, BANK OF ADAM SMITH . . .

Wait a minute! The name of every financial institution in town is listed on that panel. *What* goes on here?

Without warning, he pivots around in his chair and glowers.

"It's about time you got here!" he roars. "You trainees are all alike. Slow and bumbling . . . slow and bumbling . . ."

"But —" you stammer.

"But nothing!" he yells. "Sit down and listen. First, we work only on weekends, when the banks are closed. Second, this board gets treated with respect — understand? Respect!"

You nod but he keeps right on yelling.

"This board can shut off any burglar alarm in any bank in this town. The switches are all labeled, so I don't want no mixups. Got it? And third, these monitors will show you where the action is."

The action is on PAGE 12, got it? PAGE 12.

"I suppose that stupid cat of yours is a brainless robot, too," you say to Larena.

Your remark has the desired effect. Her eyes gleam almost as brightly as the slim dagger she pulls from her sleeve.

She moves like a flash of light toward you, but you're ready. As she thrusts the knife toward your heart, you grab her arms, forcing her into the chair.

With your left hand, you punch up 4-7-2 on Teletype No. 4 — the code you heard Larena saying in the newsroom, when she was talking on the cat's collar.

Larena stops struggling, and you call the police.

When they arrive, she is sitting in the chair, her face as expressionless as Derk's or Eban's.

"Okay, kid, what's with her?" asks the policeman.

"Job burnout, I think," you reply.

"Not funny, kid," says the officer.

"You're right," you say. "But I do have a funny story to tell you. Tonight, sir, you and I are going to save this entire country from an army of plundering robots."

"Now, that's funny!" says the officer, laughing. "Tell me about it."

THE END

You go through the green door and enter a large, brightly lit room. A trim woman, wearing a glamorous silver jumpsuit, is seated at a desk, her back to you.

"I said Code 4-7-2!" she says. "Instructions are on Teletype No. 4." She flips her silver blond hair emphatically.

She must be on the phone, you think. Your new jogging shoes are very quiet, and you feel as though you're eavesdropping. You start to back out.

Mrreeeooooww!

The strangled screech makes you jump. The woman whirls around, revealing a large gray cat standing on her desk — back arched, ready to spring.

"Who are you?" she asks, gathering the cat into her arms.

"The Career Counseling student," you reply. "I'm sorry if I interrupted your call . . ." Your voice trails off. You notice she's not holding the phone at all.

Who was she talking to? The cat?

"I'm so sorry," she says, smiling. "I didn't expect you. I told my boss I didn't have time to see you. But as long as you're here, let me introduce myself. I'm Larena — the news chief and commentator — and this is Argenta, my faithful friend."

The cat purrs as she strokes it lovingly.

If Larena and her cat haven't flipped you out by now, flip over to PAGE 52.

Following the blue footprints, you stride the length of the hallway and turn the corner. The footprints stop in front of an ordinary door.

Probably an office, you think, as you turn the brass knob.

The interior is dark, so you step inside and feel along the wall for a light switch. The door closes behind you.

The room is very small. Suddenly, the floor starts to move. You're in an elevator, and you're going down! The inside doorknob must be the control.

Silently, the elevator stops its descent, and the wall facing you slides back. In front of you, in a subterranean studio, a man is working at a control board. He is wearing a navy T-shirt that has BUTCH printed on the back.

On the wall is a neatly lettered sign:

FINANCIAL DISTRICT ALARM
CONTROL SYSTEM

What's going on here? You're curious.

If you're curious enough to get out of the elevator, turn to PAGE 25.

If you decide you can live without knowing, turn to PAGE 31.

You turn off the monitor, pick up the phone on the desk, and punch in the number of police headquarters, keeping your eye on the door every minute.

You've had just enough time to explain the situation to the police when Betsy reenters the office. She raises an eyebrow at finding you on the phone and quickly checks her bank of screens.

Think fast! She suspects you're up to something! You'll just have to fake your way through this situation.

Smiling innocently, you speak into the receiver with the dial tone humming in your ear.

"Okay, Mom. . . . Oh, yes. I'll eat lunch. . . . Oh, everyone's super. There are some real interesting people here. . . . I'll see you tonight. . . . Bye. . . ."

"Don't bet on it," says Betsy coldly, as you hang up. "Come with me."

The police said they'd come immediately. Maybe you should stall.

If you go with Betsy, turn to PAGE 10.
If you stall until the police arrive, turn to PAGE 54.

You wander down the hall and realize that you are following the trail of blue footprints. It occurs to you that Betsy probably doesn't tell the truth very often. You wonder if they really do lead to the broom closet.

Might as well check it out.

You stride toward the blue door and cautiously twist the knob.

"Welcome," says a voice with a heavy accent. "I've been waiting for you."

The man is seated at a large mahogany desk, and he sounds just like the man on the phone in the lobby.

"Come," he says, beckoning to you. "Sit down. Betsy tells me you listen very carefully."

There is an ominous ring to his words. Something weird is going on here. Maybe you should leave. Now.

"Don't leave," he says, reading your mind. "Sit down. I am Paschal, manager of KESP-TV."

Turn to PAGE 8.

You suspect that you have seen something you should not have seen when the elevator door opened.

Quickly, you step back into the elevator just as Butch swings around in his chair.

He does not look pleased to see you.

You grab the doorknob and the wall slowly starts to slide shut. Too slowly.

Butch's revolver has a silencer.

Whatever it is you have seen, you'll never talk about it.

THE END

The trail of yellow footprints ends at a yellow door. You wonder if it is a cloakroom.

You try the door. It is locked.

This is a poor beginning for anyone looking for stardom.

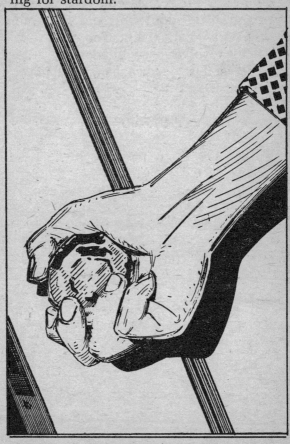

Go back to PAGE 7 and make another choice. This time, don't be so cautious.

Years after your heist, as you and Butch are lounging on the white sand outside your Hawaiian condo, you reminisce about how you stumbled into your prosperous career in crime.

"There's just one question," you say. "KESP-TV was a legitimate business. How did you ever get to use their studio and transmitter?"

"I had a trade-off going with management," Butch replies. "Their ratings were down. I convinced them that if they let me use their auxiliary transmitter to interrupt the bank alarm circuits, then they'd get to scoop all the other stations on the robberies. If it hadn't been for me, they'd never have been first with the news."

"Business deal, huh?"

"Strictly business," says Butch, reaching for his ice-cold lemonade. "You know, I've advanced a lot of careers in my time."

"You and Mrs. Downing," you reply, as you head for the surf.

THE END

You're in luck! The upstairs hall is deserted. You dash out of the elevator, down the hall, through the lobby, and out to the street. You hail a passing cab and instruct the driver to take you to the police station.

The next day, your picture is on the front page of the local paper. The headline says:

Student Scuttles Sinister
Scenario at KESP-TV

The mayor sends you a congratulatory telegram.

Mrs. Downing sends you a new Career assignment.

The taxicab company sends you a bill for $7.35.

THE END

She pushes you down the hall and stops in front of the studio door.

"Go in, Star!" she says sarcastically.

"But they're on the air!" you protest, pointing at the glowing red light above the door.

"Go in!" she snaps, giving you a shove.

"And here is our special guest now!" you hear a man say.

Bright lights blind you momentarily, and you squint in the direction of his voice. "The special student chosen for the KESP-TV Career Work Opportunity!"

The man is seated in an easy chair on a set, and he beckons for you to come and sit in the chair beside him.

The camera rolls toward you.

You glance over your shoulder. Larena is gone.

You're still close to the door. Should you run? This may be your last chance to escape these nuts!

On the other hand, it may be your first chance to star on TV!

Going to run? Turn to PAGE 72.

Going to smile for the camera? Turn to PAGE 81.

You and Betsy enter a wide hall that has several brightly colored doors down one side. Colored footprints in matching hues lead to each door. You can't believe it! This is kindergarten stuff!

Betsy sees your frown and laughs. "It's done for the tours that come through," she explains. "It keeps people from wandering into places where they shouldn't be."

"Oh," you reply, wishing that she hadn't been able to read your mind so accurately.

"Green is the newsroom, red is the main studio, and yellow is my weather-watch room," she continues.

"And the blue?" you ask.

"The blue is the decorator's joke," says Betsy, grinning. "It leads to the broom closet."

She pushes open the yellow door, and you enter a room with a large drafting table, a cluttered desk, a file cabinet, and a bank of small television screens.

Continue on PAGE 37.

"Well," Betsy says. "What would you like to know about meteorology?"

Your attention is riveted on the monitors. One is labeled LOCAL, and you stare at the cloudy low-pressure system centered over your town. A blurry picture is struggling into focus on another screen.

"No questions?" she asks.

"Just one," you reply. "What did you mean on the phone when you said, 'No tornadoes yet.' It sounded as if you could make one happen."

Her pretty, smiling face turns into an angry, rigid mask. As she starts to reply, the phone rings.

"Excuse me," she says, coldly. "Wait in the hall."

Now you've done it! You back out of the room, but as you do, you see a picture snap into view on the monitor. A man wearing an astronaut's suit is seated at a complex control board.

Impossible! you think. The man seems to be in a spaceship! What's going on here, anyway?

Want Betsy to explain what's going on? Turn to PAGE 23 (and good luck).

Want to explore the rest of the station, and forget you saw anything? Turn to PAGE 30.

Mrs. Downing shakes her head as she replies.

"No, I've served my purpose here. All I needed was one bright student to flush this pair out of hiding. And you did that!"

You smile at the compliment and feel obliged to respond.

"I'll miss you in the Career Counseling class," you say, trying to look sincere.

She stares at you sternly and frowns.

"Who are you tryin' to kid?" she snarls. "That class was *dumb*."

THE END

"And how are your brains going to master this country?" you ask Larena.

"At 9:00 tonight," she replies, with a hint of triumph in her voice, "every financial institution in every city, town, and hamlet of your country will be relieved of its tangible assets."

"Mass robbery?" you ask. "How? You said your country has no manpower. No military."

"Stupid!" she snaps. "We have robot power! Thousands of Derks and Ebans are stationed across the nation — all programmed into this one panel and all awaiting my electronic instructions, which will be beamed on the KESP transmitter."

"I hate to disappoint you," you say, "but the KESP signal doesn't carry as far as Chicago. You know — snowy picture, garbled sound."

"Fool! I beam the KESP signal to our satellite, which transmits it back to the sites where my robots are waiting!"

She smiles threateningly and moves closer. "My robots are very lifelike, don't you think?" Her voice drops to a whisper. "But they don't bleed. It will be a bloodless victory."

If you think it's time to say bye-bye to the robot lady, flip over to PAGE 84.

If you think it's your patriotic duty to stop her crazy plan, turn to PAGE 26.

You pull out your Swiss Army knife and slip one of the blades between the lock and the frame. The drawer slides open easily, revealing a small white metal box with pink flowers enameled on its sides. A label in front says: RECIPES.

Recipes? you think angrily. What kind of espionage is this?

You open the box and flip through the cards.

Aunt Mamie's Sourdough Bread . . . English Cottage Stew . . . Homemade Tornadoes . . . Chocolate Cream Pudd —

Wait a minute! Homemade Tornadoes? You pull the card.

AF 1 RECEPTION: HOMEMADE TORNADOES
    Take warm moist air at ground level.
    Force cold dry air on top.
    Go 3-7-9   Abort 5-1-2

Today's date and 1500 appear in the upper right corner.

You are puzzling over your find when the door flies open.

"So now you know," Betsy snaps, pointing a revolver at you. "Come with me. You are too nosy for your own good!"

If you know how to defuse a tornado, turn to PAGE 49.

If you're not sure how you'll survive this squall, turn to PAGE 67.

Lt. Col. Betsy Boggitt! Who does she think she's kidding? The entire KESP-TV staff is probably having a great laugh right now — at your expense!

Well, you're not going to be anybody's stooge!

You stomp out into the hall, clutching the note, just in time to see Betsy being led through the door to the lobby by a man holding a gun.

She wasn't kidding! You must do something!

"Fire!" you yell. "Fire in the control room!"

The man pivots around at the sound of your voice, but before he can shoot, Betsy kicks the gun from his hand.

Kick over to PAGE 85.

You pull the pepperoni from your pocket and sit down on the floor in front of the teletype, looking up at Argenta. The cat sniffs suspiciously from her perch, then gracefully leaps down. In seconds, she is climbing into your lap to reach the meat stick in your hand.

As you stroke her fur, your finger catches on her collar. There is a burst of static and a man's voice says: "Come in, 3-2-9."

Startled, you examine Argenta's jeweled neck strap. This is no ordinary collar. It has batteries and wires inside, like a radio. Now you know why Larena wasn't using the phone! She was sending orders to someone on this strange two-way radio!

You press down on one of the decorative jewels. The static abruptly ceases.

"All right, snoop!" Larena's sharp voice cuts the silence. "On your feet! Come with me! I told my boss getting a student in here was a bad move. But he said it would look good if the station did some public service. So much for that!"

You have no idea how long she's been in the room. And that silver revolver in her hand means business. She snaps her fingers, and the big cat leaps to her shoulder.

It's your move. What are you going to do?

Going with Larena? Turn to PAGE 35.
Going to resist? Turn to PAGE 19.

You turn and leap for the lobby door just as Mrs. Downing fires.

"If I've told you once, I've told you a hundred times," she yells as you sink to the floor. "Follow instructions! You'll get an F for this!"

"Who are you really?" you ask in a weak voice.

"Dolly Downing," she replies harshly, looking down at you. "Career Counseling teacher."

"I mean *really*," you gasp, testily.

"Does it really matter?" she replies.

"I guess not," you whisper.

Your career at KESP-TV has been terminated.

THE END

"I'm the station custodian," you say, quickly sizing up the situation. "I'm here to clean this place up!"

"Don't put me on, kid. The staff wouldn't let a custodian down here. It's their necks, too. I'm pirating signals off the transmitter to run my board. They get a cut."

"I don't know what you're talking about," you say, looking Butch straight in the eye. "This is my first day on the job, and I told the manager I'd clean the place from top to bottom, and that's what I'm going to do! Now, where's the utility closet?"

"There ain't no closet down here!" Butch yells.

That is exactly what you expect to hear.

"Then I'll have to go back upstairs to get my equipment," you announce, heading for the elevator.

"You ain't goin' nowhere, kid!" Butch bellows, lunging for you. "You've seen too much."

Your timing is perfect. Butch trips over your foot and lands flat on his face.

When he stumbles, you dart into the elevator and twist the knob. It silently ascends to the first floor.

Silently turn back to PAGE 34.

You place the list of meteorological terms down on the desk and move stealthily to the ex-Bishop weather station monitor. The weather station may be phased out, but somebody is transmitting, because you saw that astronaut. You're going to get to the bottom of this.

You push the ON button, and a picture snaps into focus. You see the same astronaut in front of the same electronic panel. He is working feverishly, pushing buttons and pulling handles. His uniform is different from those of the United States astronauts you've seen on television. Maybe he's from a foreign country, but which one? — and what is he doing?

Should you try to track down a KESP security person? See if you can find some high executive to check things out? Call the police? Or just wait a bit and try to snoop a little more?

Going to grab that phone? Turn to PAGE 29.

Going to snoop around some more? Turn to PAGE 79.

"Good move!" says Paschal, reading your mind. "You will work with me on tonight's show when I interview James Delman of the Urban Art Museum."

"But what will I do?" you ask.

(For once, he didn't answer you before you asked the question.)

"Betsy will train you this afternoon," he replies.

The training is unlike any you have had before. You are locked in a sky blue room and hypnotized. As you recline on a leather couch, taped video lessons are played through a monitor. At the end of the tape you are asked to identify and predict pictures and cards *before* they are shown. You correctly guess all of them.

Five minutes before show time, Paschal comes to get you.

"You will be in this control room next to the set," he says. "You must be close to the person whose mind you are reading. You are to record whatever thoughts come from Mr. Delman's mind."

It all sounds like a game to you.

"This is no game!" snaps Paschal. (There he goes again.) "It is time you capitalized on your great talent."

He hands you a notepad, then leaves. You feel uneasy. Is he going to do something illegal?

You may legally turn to PAGE 74.

"Here, kitty, kitty," you purr at the hissing cat.

You lay the pepperoni stick down on the floor in front of the machine. Argenta eyes it suspiciously but refuses to be lured from her perch.

This is ridiculous! you think.

You have it all figured out. The teletype can't possibly have an electrical short, or Larena wouldn't let her cat perch on its top. That would be too dangerous.

Besides, you know this is the mysterious Teletype No. 4 that she was talking about. What could the instructions be?

Hissing back at Argenta, you mutter: "If I go, you go, too, you dumb cat!"

In one swift motion, you swing the ruler up to hit the toggle switch. The machine leaps into noisy activity. Argenta leaps into the air.

And you? You sink to the floor as the surge of electricity is conducted through the metal ruler into your body.

You forgot one thing. Argenta has nine lives.

You only have one.

THE END

Your hand closes tightly around a potted plant on the desk. You throw it at Betsy with one clean, swift motion. The gun flies from her hand and lands on the floor.

"Sit down," you order, picking up the gun and pointing it at her. As you speak, the phone rings.

"Answer it," you command. "And no tricks. The code is 5-1-2. Got it? 5-1-2."

"Hello," she says.

You press the gun to her temple and whisper, "5-1-2."

"5-1-2," she repeats. "Code 5-1-2." She hangs up and smirks. "It's too late," she says. "They've already seeded the upper air."

"Dial the air base," you say. "Ask for the commander."

She dials slowly and asks for the commander. You grab the phone.

"Commander? I am working at KESP-TV and have good reason to believe that the people running this studio are part of a deadly plot to assassinate the President. You must tell me: Is Air Force One coming in at your base at 1500 hours?"

There is a sputtering noise. "How did you know that?" the commander demands. "It's a military secret!"

"It's a long story. Listen!"

You tell him everything.

Continue on PAGE 50.

The commander acts immediately. "I'll be there in fifteen minutes," he tells you. "Keep your suspect under guard until I arrive with the air police."

The commander and his officers are there in less than fifteen minutes. It's a good thing, too, because you didn't know how much longer you could keep Betsy at gunpoint.

The air police handcuff Betsy and take her away. The commander assures you that he and his force have already averted the planned disaster: "One of our hurricane hunters has been dispatched to drop a silver iodide bomb into the primary energy cell of the storm," he tells you. "And Air Force One has been diverted to a different route. NASA is tracking the astronaut you saw. There's a foreign power at work here, you know. You'll be recognized for this!"

Later that month, a dinner is held in your honor. The President herself acknowledges your heroism.

"You did a brave thing," she says, shaking your hand. "On behalf of the citizens of this country, I am offering you a coveted slot at the Air Force Academy, where you will study with the best youth of our nation! Well, what do you say?"

You think for a moment before you reply.

"Will I have to take a Career Counseling class?" you ask.

THE END

"Luscious Larena's an enemy agent," says Hobart Huckle. "She's been sent to sabotage the communications system of the country through the KESP-TV transmitter."

He points to a door marked KEEP OUT.

"If she gets in there to the transmitter panel, she'll scramble every signal from Vero Beach, Florida, to Coos Bay, Oregon. Your job is to keep her out."

"How am I supposed to do that?" you ask indignantly. "She's got a gun!"

"She wouldn't dare kill you here," Hobart replies. "She knows that might make me suspicious."

"I hope so," you mutter.

"Now get back in there and stick to her like glue until I can find out if she has accomplices around here."

"She does!" you say. "She talks to them on her cat's collar!"

"Sure, kid," says Hobart, steering you toward the newsroom. For a moment you hesitate — and look down the hall at the lobby door!

Going to make another run for it? Dash over to PAGE 68.

Going to give Hobart Huckle the help he so obviously needs? Hike over to PAGE 70.

52

"Let's learn about the wire services," says Larena, moving toward a noisy bank of teletype machines. "These two give us world and national news, and this one has regional news and feature stories."

"What about this one?" you ask, pointing to an idle machine.

You have barely spoken when, with a fierce roar, Argenta leaps at you.

Larena pales. "No. 4 is broken," she says curtly, taking her cat from your shoulders. She sets the animal down on top of the No. 4 machine. "It has an electrical short. Argenta sleeps on it. She thinks it's hers."

There's something fishy about all this. You know she was talking to somebody about instructions on Teletype No. 4.

You notice that the toggle switch is in the OFF position.

"I have a newscast to do now," Larena says, looking at the clock. "Don't disturb Argenta — and don't turn on that teletype!"

She leaves, and you approach the machine. In one hand is an 18-inch metal ruler that you've taken from her desk. The other hand is curled around the pepperoni stick you have in your pocket for a quick snack.

Argenta hisses and arches her back.

If you turn on Teletype No. 4, turn to PAGE 48.

If you make friends with Argenta, turn to PAGE 42.

"Fast thinking!" Larena says to you. "The general was given a truth serum. He was about to reveal some classified material."

"What were you doing with the transmitter?" you ask.

"Trying to disable it before the general spilled the beans," she replies cheerfully. "But the auxiliary power came on immediately. If it hadn't been for you, the country would be in terrible trouble!"

You lean down to stroke Argenta, who has wandered into the studio. "And what about her collar?" you ask.

"My hook-up to headquarters," Larena explains. "I'm Agent Larena Luscious, assigned to the Midwest office."

"The teletype?" you ask.

"My direct link with the White House."

"Why did you pull a gun on me?" you demand.

"I thought you might be Hobart in disguise."

"I don't get it," you say. "Why would Hobart be dumb enough to broadcast classified material publicly? Then everybody would hear it."

"You're too smart to ask a dumb question like that," Larena says, frowning. "Tell me, how many people do you know who watch talk shows on Saturday afternoons?"

She's got a point.

THE END

"I didn't know there were so many kinds of clouds," you say to Betsy, ignoring her command to leave the weather studio. You point to the paper with the definitions she told you to study. "Cumulo-nimbus, cirrus, nimbo-stratus, noctilucent, nacreous —"

"Save your breath!" she snaps. "I told you not to touch the equipment — and that includes the phones. If you can't follow instructions, you can't work here! You're in big trouble!"

"Or maybe you are, lady."

Betsy whirls around to face the policeman standing in the doorway. Beside him is a military police officer from the nearby air base.

"Why?" she asks.

"We got a report about an astronaut in foreign uniform showing up on one of your monitors," he continues. "We'd like to know more about it."

"Certainly," she says, flipping the switch on what used to be the Bishop weather station monitor.

The astronaut appears on the screen. He seems to be talking to himself as he punches buttons and pulls levers.

"Would you like audio as well as video?" Betsy asks.

To learn what the astronaut says, turn to PAGE 89.

You stare at the piece of yellow news-print.

Hobart Huckle, foreign espionage agent and master of disguise, escaped last night from the federal penitentiary and is believed to be hiding in the area. Huckle outwitted his guards by posing as the warden of the prison. A reward is offered . . .

You glance over at Larena. So she thinks you have no nose for news! Well, you'll show her!

"I have a scoop," you announce, calmly but clearly.

"Really," she replies in a bored voice, without looking up.

"Yes," you say. "Hobart Huckle, espionage agent and master of disguise, is in this very building, preparing to go on the air as Hobart Hansom, television talk show host."

"Do tell," says Larena. "Well, Hobart is a common enough name. You must be confused. Why would you think it's the same person?"

All Hobarts turn to PAGE 1 and start over.
Everyone else continue reading on PAGE 56.

"He told me," you reply to Larena. "In the hall —"

"I see," says Larena. "An enemy agent introduced himself to you in the hall."

"Just a minute ago," you say triumphantly. "That *is* a scoop, isn't it?"

"That *was* a minute ago," says Larena. "Where is he now?"

"He's right here at KESP-TV!" you yell. "In the studio! I'll find him!"

"Do that," she says, turning back to her typewriter.

"I will!" you shout, bolting from your desk. You wrench open the door and run down the hall toward the studio.

Larena's silvery laugh follows you. You turn just in time to see her slip into the hall, take a key from her charm bracelet, and unlock the door to the transmitter panel.

Tricked!

"Stick to her like glue," Hobart told you.

That news release must have been a phony. Or was it?

Which one is KESP's fallen star?

Larena? Turn to PAGE 63.
Hobart? Turn to PAGE 71.

"I'm sorry you have chosen to leave," says Paschal, reading your thoughts even before you tell him of your decision. "I must ask you to go immediately. Do not worry about completing your school assignment. You will be given a fair grade."

He ushers you out to the lobby, while you try to keep your mind free of uncomplimentary thoughts like *weirdo*, *wacky*, and *loony bin*.

You're certainly not going to tell anyone about your experiences at KESP-TV. They'd never believe you. You suspect Paschal knows that, as well.

At the end of the term, Mrs. Downing gives you an A+ based, she tells you, on reports from the station manager. You secretly wonder what your grade would have been had you stayed.

Your brief encounter with Betsy and Paschal has a lasting effect on your future. You eventually become an eminent psychiatrist and spend the rest of your working life trying to read people's minds.

Oh, yes. And you rarely watch TV.

THE END

While the operator is putting the call through, you drag the phone out of the bugged room, into the hall. The cord is just long enough to reach.

Col. Corkley comes on the line immediately.

"Tornado Project," he says. "Corkley here."

"I'm a student working at KESP-TV. Betsy Boggitt is in danger. She asked me to tell you that she's been taken to Death Valley!" you say.

"When?"

"Thirty minutes ago," you reply.

"We'll send planes from Nellis and ground troops from Fort Irwin," he says. "This country is indebted to you. You'll get a reward for this!"

The dial tone hums in your ear as you lean back and wonder what your reward will be.

In June, there is a special ceremony at your school. Betsy is there and Col. Corkley comes from the Pentagon.

You are presented with the deed to the defunct Bishop weather station. Nothing could please you more. You have lost interest in the "glamorous" world of television. You're on your way to becoming a world-famous meteorologist!

THE END

"Not me!" you say to Larena. "I'm not going underground for anybody!"

You're almost positive now that her credentials are phony, and you suspect that she only wants to use you as a hostage.

The desk moves again with an ominous, rasping scrape.

"Suit yourself," she snaps, lowering herself into the hole.

She pushes a button and the teletype machine glides noiselessly into place. That's when you notice Argenta's collar on the floor. Just as you pick it up, Hobart comes crashing into the room.

He stands facing you — gun drawn, expression hostile. In the hallway beyond, you see two armed men flanking the door.

"She went thataway," you say.

"Forget her, kid," Hobart snarls. "Just hand me the collar, nice and easy."

You look at the jeweled strap in your hand. *Why is it so special?* you wonder.

"Now!" snaps Hobart. "Give it to me now! Carefully!"

"What's the big deal?" you ask, handing it over.

Hobart frowns. "I ask the questions around here," he says. "I want to make sure you really are a student. You got any ID? Empty your pockets!"

You don't have much choice. Turn to PAGE 60.

60

You empty your pockets as Hobart watches.

Wallet, comb, three sticks of cherry gum, bus pass, four raisins, last week's science test, and seventy-two cents.

"Okay, okay," says Hobart. "That's enough. I believe you."

"Thanks," you reply. "Now, what's with the cat's collar?"

"If these jewels are depressed in a certain sequence," says Hobart, "an explosive device at one of our satellite stations will be detonated. Then we'd *really* have a communications problem."

He cautiously hands the collar out to the men in the hall.

"Take it to headquarters," Hobart orders.

"Aren't you going after Larena?" you ask.

"No. I know about her secret tunnel. I have men stationed at the other end. I'm going back to the studio. The auxiliary transmitter's operating now. KESP's back on the air."

He leans over and winks. "I like this television business even better than the FBI," he says, smoothing his hair. "I'm hosting the evening talk show, and you're going to do the next newscast — so get to work!"

This is it. Your TV debut. You're going to be a Star!

You hope Mrs. Downing is watching.

THE END

Twelve hours after the tornado has struck, rescue crews find you, still in the broom closet, which has been blown to the edge of a cornfield.

When you try to tell them that Betsy and the astronaut created the tornado to destroy Air Force One and the President, they sedate you and take you to the nearest hospital.

"The President is safe," the doctor reassures you, in a patronizing tone.

He does not tell you until weeks later that you are the only survivor from KESP-TV.

Eventually, you stop trying to convince people of the sinister doings at KESP-TV. But twenty years later, you write a book called *Betsy's Homemade Tornado.*

It is a best-seller.

You win a Pulitzer Prize.

For fiction.

THE END

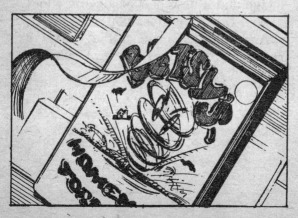

You splash down the alley and hail a passing patrol car. You have trouble convincing the policemen that two robots are robbing the bank, but when the officers finally get inside, their skepticism disappears.

Derk is sitting motionless in front of the vault, while Eban dangles from the skylight. As you suspected, the Laser Box contains their control programs, through which Larena choreographs their actions.

You have singlefootedly cracked the Case of the Printless Thieves — one that has baffled the city police for months!

Larena and Hobart, who have been using the KESP-TV transmitter to relay commands to the robots, are picked up as they are boarding a flight for South America.

A dinner is held in your honor. The police commissioner gives you an honorary badge and a new pair of jogging shoes.

Mrs. Downing gives you an A+.

And you give a speech that starts, "The real world of work is not what you imagine . . ."

THE END

You turn and sprint back toward Larena. Your new jogging shoes serve you well, but not well enough. You are just three strides away when a blinding flash of light rips through the control panel.

"That's that," says Larena, dusting off her hands.

"You tricked me!" you yell. "What else do you have up your sleeve?"

"This," she replies, slipping a silver gun into her hand. "Now march right back into the newsroom and be quick! Your future is at stake. Hobart will kill us."

"*Us?*" you yell. "He's not after me! I'm his deputy!"

The words are barely spoken when Hobart appears in the studio doorway.

"Don't go with her!" he yells, waving a gun.

"Get into the newsroom!" Larena says, nudging her gun into the small of your back.

Staying with Hobart? Turn to PAGE 64.
Going with Larena? Turn to PAGE 73.

Hobart fires a shot over Larena's head. You knock the gun from her hand and drop to the floor.

"Get her, Hobie!" you yell, as Larena shoves open the newsroom door.

You look up. Hobart is aiming at you!

"Sorry, kid," he snarls.

You close your eyes. This is it. You're a sitting duck. Larena's gun is just out of reach.

Mmmrrrrreeooowwww!

You open one eye. You'd know that noise anywhere. Argenta, streaking through the newsroom doorway, covers the length of the hall and disarms Hobart with one leap.

You open two eyes. Two uniformed policemen are entering from the lobby. They grab Hobart and handcuff him.

"Nice work, Captain," says one.

"Captain?" you whisper, turning to look at Larena.

She nods slowly.

You quickly review the past sixty seconds. Aiding and abetting a criminal. Disarming a police officer. Obstructing an officer in the performance of duty. Disobeying a police officer. Being saved by a *cat*. That's the most humiliating of all.

You suspect that this may be the end of your TV career.

Check your suspicions on PAGE 66.

"Hobart was about to broadcast classified information in code," Larena explains. "Information too important to be sent by courier. I had to destroy the transmitter to stop him. He had accomplices in the studio and control room."

"I get it!" you say eagerly, hoping she'll forget that you weren't exactly helpful. "He figured the viewers wouldn't know it was classified and only the enemy agents could decipher it."

"Exactly!" says Larena. "That's very clever of you."

"You were talking to the policemen on Argenta's collar, right?"

"Right!" she says. "Very clever deduction."

You stare down at your new jogging shoes. If she thinks you're that clever, maybe you can push your luck.

"The news release says there's a reward for Hobart," you say greedily. "After all, I was the one who told you he was here. What do I get for that?"

Larena stares at you coldly through steely blue eyes.

"C-minus," she snaps. "And only because I'm having a good day."

THE END

Betsy marches you down the hall to the broom closet.

"Inside," she snaps. "And give me that knife."

You have no choice. A key clicks in the lock. When you're sure she's gone, you search the closet for something that will help you escape. Pails, mops, brooms, a ladder — what's this?!

A transistor radio! It must belong to one of the janitors. With fumbling fingers, you turn it on.

"At the top of the news: The President's plane, Air Force One, will make an unscheduled landing in our city at 3:00 P.M. The President's unexpected arrival has caught city officials unprepared. . . . In weather news: Unpredictable weather patterns continue over the area. Present temperature is 85 degrees; humidity, 93 percent. . . ."

That's it! Betsy knew the President was coming. Maybe she created the killer tornado to assassinate her!

You rattle the door and pound on the walls, but no one comes. It's useless. You sit down and rest your head on the wall. The closet is warm and dark . . . and the music is soft and sweet. You fall asleep.

Wake up and get over to PAGE 61.

You twist from Hobart's grasp and sprint toward the door. Your action catches him off guard. Before he has time to react, you are through the door and safely in the lobby.

"What took you so long?" says a familiar voice.

You turn slowly to face the speaker.

It's Mrs. Downing, and she's holding a gun!

"Hurry!" she says, as she runs across the room.

She reaches up and twists one of the blue light bulbs on the wall. As she does, a panel in the wall slides open, revealing a room full of complicated machinery.

"Get in there!" she commands you. "They'll be here any minute!"

Want to pass Career Counseling? Turn to PAGE 69.

Want to terminate your assignment? Turn to PAGE 44.

"I don't get it," you say to Mrs. Downing. "You're supposed to be a teacher!"

"Teaching is my cover," she replies as she follows you into the room. "I'm a Secret Service agent."

She pushes a button and the panel slides shut behind her.

"Then you must know Hobart! Hobart is an agent!"

"Hobart is a double agent," she says. "And Larena is his accomplice. She was talking to him on the cat's collar."

She waves her gun at the equipment.

"This is the Midwest Espionage Control Center. We knew there were spies at KESP — but we weren't sure who they were. Now we know, thanks to you."

"But aren't you going to take them in?" you ask.

"My men are picking them up now," she says. "I can't afford to be seen, or my usefulness as an agent will be over. You'll get credit for their capture. Tomorrow, I fly to Naples on a new case."

"So you won't be back at school after spring break?" you ask, trying not to sound too hopeful.

Will she? Won't she? Try PAGE 38.

Your mother always said you'd never solve anything by running away. You push open the newsroom door.

"Stick to her like glue," Hobart whispers. "She's slick." He leaves you and heads down the hall to the studio.

Larena scarcely looks up when you enter the newsroom. She is seated at a desk, typing, and Argenta is off in a corner grooming herself. The gun is nowhere in sight.

Larena rolls the page from the typewriter and swings around to face you.

"Some journalist you are!" she snaps. "If you'd had a nose for news, you'd have interviewed me to find out why I had a gun! You'll never get anywhere in this business if you run off at the least little thing!" (She sounds just like your mother.)

"I should give you an F!" she goes on. "But I'll give you one more chance. Here. Rewrite these stories. I need them for the noon news."

"Yes, ma'am," you reply, taking the news clips from her.

You sit down at the typewriter and start reading the top story. You don't get past the first sentence. This is incredible!

Incredible or not, all readers should go to PAGE 55.
Those who do not, get an F.

You look back at Larena and shrug. You're not sure what she's going to do to the transmitter, but you're sure now that Hobart was lying. Larena can't possibly foul up the whole country's communications — only the KESP broadcasts.

Hobart must think you're pretty dumb.

Ignoring the glowing red light, you enter the studio. On the set with Hobart Hansom is an army officer in full dress uniform.

"Today," Hobart says, "my guest is General Stanley McBrindle, chief of all missile sites. Welcome to KESP-TV, General."

The general turns to face Hobart, and from the glassy look in his eyes, you wonder if he's been drugged.

"Tell us about your newest missile site, General," Hobart says, smiling.

You must stop this interview. But how?

By word? Turn to PAGE 17.
By action? Turn to PAGE 91.

Forget about starring on television, you think.

Scowling at the approaching camera, you whirl around and wrench open the door. A feeling of relief washes over you. Larena is nowhere in sight. You may never know why she had a gun — or to whom she was talking on Argenta's collar — or why Teletype No. 4 was so mysterious. And you don't care. You're getting out of here!

You pause in the doorway to stick your tongue out one last time at the camera. And that's when you hear it. A tiny click, like a gun being cocked.

The weapon concealed in the camera is very quiet.

You slump to the floor. The last thing you hear is the announcer saying: "Join us next Saturday for more mystery and excitement from the studios of KESP-TV."

THE END

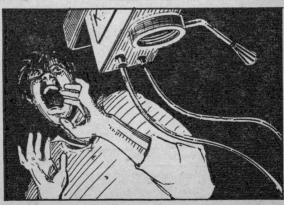

You shove open the newsroom door. Once inside, Larena slips her gun back into her sleeve.

"Hurry!" she commands. "We must block the door!"

"Why should I help you?" you ask, feeling braver now that the gun is out of sight.

"Because I'm a special agent," she snaps, producing an ID card. "Now hurry! He's gone for the others!"

The sound of running footsteps in the hall outside makes your decision easy. You put your shoulder to the heavy desk she is shoving and help her push it up against the door.

"Follow me!" she orders, running to Teletype No. 4.

With urgency, she pushes the switch to ON, and you watch as the entire machine swings aside, revealing a steep staircase into a darkened hole. This is weird.

The noise in the hall grows louder, and the desk scrapes on the floor as the door is forced open.

"Go down!" Larena commands.

Argenta jumps from the machine and scampers down the stairs.

"Hurry!" says Larena.

Going? Turn to PAGE 20.
Staying? Turn to PAGE 59.

74

You watch through the glass window of the control room as the interview begins. You pick up the pencil and notepad, waiting to receive unspoken messages from Mr. Delman's mind.

The small, elderly curator proudly tells Paschal about the jade collection that has just arrived at the museum.

"A priceless exhibit, is it not?" Paschal asks.

"Oh, yes," replies Mr. Delman. "Irreplaceable."

"And kept in the vault when the museum is closed, I would suspect," Paschal comments casually.

"Oh, yes!" Mr. Delman replies.

That's when it happens. Your hand automatically writes down a series of numbers. Mr. Delman must have subconsciously thought of the combination when Paschal mentioned the vault.

Of course! Paschal and Betsy are going to steal the jade!

Paschal looks at you sharply. He's reading your mind!

Is this a path to quick riches for you . . . or a road to the slammer?

So what are you thinking?

Going to call the cops? Turn to PAGE 11.
Going to get rich quick? Turn to PAGE 16.

"I have a splitting headache," you say to Larena. "Maybe I should just stay here."

"Of course," she says sweetly. "Just lean back and close your eyes."

You lean back, but you don't close your eyes. Thoughts of a cat's collar and a studio and camera float through your mind. You watch as she punches up a combination of numbers on the control board. Derk and Eban move stiffly — mechanically — toward the door. When Derk opens it, you squint to see the gold-lettered sign on its front panel. It says:

ROBOTICS AND DEPROGRAMMING

You gasp, and Larena looks at you sharply. "I said close your eyes!" she snaps, turning quickly to the board to punch some more numbers.

You feel a warm sensation creeping up your arms, and you instantly lift them from the armrests. At the same time, you raise your head from the leather headrest. This chair is wired! But why? Are they going to torture you? Brainwash you? You know one thing. No one's going to control your mind!

If you jump and run, turn to PAGE 78.

If you get out of the chair but stay in the room to satisfy your curiosity, turn to PAGE 24.

You grab the wheel from Eban and wrench it hard. The van veers into the path of the police car, which screeches to a halt just inches away.

You reach across Derk and open the door, crawling over him to get out.

"Boy, am I glad to see you!" you shout at the policemen.

"The feeling's mutual," drawls one. "We just got the report."

"Report?" you ask, puzzled.

"Report!" he repeats. "Report that some dumb kid was joyriding in the KESP-TV remote truck. Get into the squad car!"

"I didn't steal it!" you shout. "I was sent with Eban and Derk. They're robots. They're right there in the cab!"

But even as you turn to point, you know that Larena has won. There is no one in the cab. Derk and Eban have disappeared. On the seat are two metal boxes, each marked: REMOTE UNIT — PROPERTY OF KESP-TV. The Laser Box is gone.

Later that day, in the holding cell at the county jail, you watch your capture on the KESP-TV evening news.

Not exactly what you had in mind for your TV debut.

THE END

Staying close to the building, out of range of the box, you run to the end of the alley. As you reach the street, the wail of sirens fills the air. Patrol cars and motorcycle police whiz by. One car stops and an officer gets out.

"Hurry!" you yell. "A pair of robots is robbing the bank!"

"Think you can stall us, huh, kid?" says the policeman. "You must be the decoy! When the silent alarm went off, we figured it was another job of the Phantom Thieves — always on a Saturday and never a trace of evidence. It's a smooth operation!"

"I'm no decoy and they're not gone!" you yell. "They're right over there filming the whole thing. Search that van!"

"You're daffy," says the policeman. "That's the KESP-TV remote crew. They do a terrific job. They've been at the scene of every robbery we've had in the last two months. Sometimes even before we . . . get . . . there . . ."

His voice slows as he realizes what he is saying.

Later that month, you are honored by the local law enforcement agency and the broadcasters' union for your part in solving the Phantom Robberies.

THE END

You bolt from the chair, fling open the door, and race down the hall.

Strange, you think as you run. *Larena is making no attempt to stop you.*

At the end of the passageway, you come to a door marked DO NOT ENTER. You push it open, and as you do, a flood of bright light blinds you.

"And here is our special guest now," you hear a man say. "Welcome to the studios of KESP-TV! My name is Hobart Hansom."

He grabs your hand and as he pumps it up and down, you feel a slight prick in your palm.

This is where I came in, you think, as you lose consciousness.

Congratulations! Maybe you'll have a second chance to find out what your fate would have been with Derk and Eban.

Meanwhile, there's no question about it . . . this is

THE END

You know you shouldn't snoop, but you'll never get to the bottom of this astronaut business if you don't.

You pull open one of the drawers in Betsy's desk and rifle through the contents. One stale cheese sandwich, two cookies, a bottle of perfume.

You try the middle drawer. Now you're getting warm! A map! A map of the United States with a line drawn between Washington, D.C., and the air base just outside your town. *That's pretty strange.* At the top of the map is today's date and 1500 hours.

You know that 1500 means 3:00 P.M.

You consult your watch. It's 12:10.

Is something going to happen at 3:00 — something that involves the air base, Washington, Betsy, tornadoes, and that astronaut? You'd better snoop some more.

You tug at the upper left drawer. It's locked.

Turn to PAGE 40.

As Paschal hands you and Betsy each a tray of the precious stones, you sense, rather than hear, someone behind you.

Betsy gasps, and you turn to see Mr. Delman standing there, flanked by two burly officers holding guns.

"How did you know?" Paschal snarls, raising his hands over his head.

Mr. Delman smiles amiably.

"My horoscope told me not to trust curious strangers today. Astrology is a much older art than mind reading."

You don't have to be a mind reader to know what your future will bring.

You, Betsy, and Paschal each get ten years in the poky.

You flunk Career Counseling.

THE END

You smooth your hair and smile for the approaching camera as you walk toward the set. You hope Mrs. Downing and your classmates are watching.

"Good afternoon," you say to the man, as you sit in the easy chair. "It's nice to be here." Your diction is perfect.

"We're very glad to have you with us," he replies. "Welcome to the studios of KESP-TV. My name is Hobart Hansom."

You feel a slight prick in your palm as you reach over to shake his outstretched hand, and within seconds you slump over in the easy chair. As you lose consciousness, you hear Larena's voice: "Code 4-7-2 . . . Code 4-7-2 . . ." She must be talking on Argenta's collar again.

So much for your TV debut.

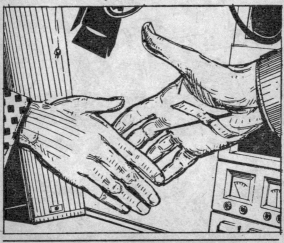

Continue reading on PAGE 83.

When you regain consciousness, you are sitting in a strange chair — almost like a dentist's chair — in a windowless room. Against a wall you can see several control boards.

Larena is bending over you with an expression of concern. Standing behind her are two well-built men.

"Feeling better?" she asks solicitously. "You fainted in the studio. It must have been the lights and the excitement. I think you need some fresh air. I've assigned you to the remote crew for the afternoon."

She gestures toward the men. "Eban and Derk will show you what to do. They'll be covering the Grand Opening of the First National Bank and Trust."

She smiles slyly, and you look over at Eban and Derk. Expressionless, they return your stare. Your mind seems hazy. There's something wrong here. Aren't the banks closed on Saturday? *Is this Saturday?* You can't remember.

Your head is throbbing.

Going with Derk and Eban? Turn to PAGE 13.

Going to plead illness? Turn to PAGE 75.

You lunge for the door, jerk it open, and run down the hall. Your heart races as you leap up a flight of stairs and fling open the door at the top.

Fresh air! You try to breathe deeply, but your lungs don't respond. Everything looks strange. Without success, you struggle to remember where you've been and where you're going. It's as if you've lost all your human feelings. You don't notice the sultry summer drizzle that's soaking your shirt. Mechanically, you walk down the street and turn the corner.

The van is waiting. Eban and Derk wave as you get closer, and you wave back at your new friends, awkwardly.

Don't worry about it. It will take time for your new stainless steel joints to move freely. Larena will reprogram your hinges when you get back to her Robotics Laboratory.

Meanwhile, dry yourself off before you rust.

You and Derk and Eban are off for an unscheduled grand opening of the First National vault.

They'll never catch you. You don't leave fingerprints.

THE END

"You've saved your country!" Betsy says, as she subdues the man who had held her captive. "You'll get a gold medal for this!"

In the autumn of that year, a special ceremony is held in your honor. You sit up on the platform, surrounded by dignitaries, while your family, Mrs. Downing, and your classmates watch you being honored.

After a long and boring speech, the Chief of Staff pins a bronze medal on your shoulder.

You lean over to Betsy. "I thought you said it would be gold," you whisper.

"Sorry about that," she whispers back. "But you slipped up."

"Slipped up?" you repeat in astonishment. "How?"

"You forgot to do the filing," she replies.

THE END

86

You've never been noted for patience.

"Brains are weapons," you say to Larena, smiling. "And it obviously took a master brain to design this control panel."

"It is my design!" she announces proudly. "All mine!"

"What does that green switch control?" you ask, pointing to an unmarked lever on her right.

Your trick works! She turns to see what you are pointing to.

"The green is—"

Before she can finish the sentence, you yank down the orange MASTER lever. Nothing happens.

"The green is," she repeats, "the master."

She turns to face you. She is holding a small gun.

"The orange was a decoy," she adds.

She smiles at you, and you sigh.

"You're right, of course," she says. "Brains are weapons. Unfortunately, yours just misfired."

She is an expert shot. Her revolver does not misfire.

THE END

You climb into the backseat of the police car and lean against the cushioned upholstery. That's when you notice the small TV set into the back of the front seat. You watch in horror as the astronaut on the screen pushes buttons and pulls levers. This isn't a police car! You've been tricked!

The driver turns to you and smiles.

"You're too smart for your own good, kid," he says. "I don't think you're going to get home for dinner."

He waves at the squad car that is turning the corner, heading toward the KESP-TV studios.

"Too bad they made the trip for nothing," he says.

THE END

You look at Derk's Laser Box again and decide against doing anything heroic. To make matters worse, the policemen wave at the KESP van as it goes by.

The truck steers into a narrow, deserted alley behind the bank. Derk and Eban jump out, and you follow them to an unmarked metal door, over which a fire escape dangles. You watch in amazement as Eban places one foot on the door and effortlessly walks to the top. *His shoes must be magnetized*, you think.

It's all clear now. The Grand Opening of the bank is definitely unauthorized.

Derk pokes you. "Stay!" he commands.

He then follows Eban up the door and onto the fire escape. When he's almost to the roof, Derk stops and attaches The Box to one of the fire escape steps. You can't be sure from where you're standing, but it looks as if he is aiming it at you.

"Stay!" he repeats, disappearing over the edge of the roof.

"Don't talk to me like a dog, you dumb robot!" you mutter.

Should you chance an escape? Does The Box really contain a laser?

If you think you know what's in The Box, turn to PAGE 22.

If you feel more comfortable not even thinking about what's in The Box, turn to PAGE 77.

Betsy flips a switch and the astronaut's voice fills the office.

"Punch in some nutrition, add a little
   corn,
Pull it through a sound wave—
That's how CRUNCH is born!
Good for little astronauts,
Good for big ones, too,
That's what Cap'n Astro says—
CRUNCH is good for you!"

Everyone is staring at you.

Your astronaut is KESP's Cap'n Astro filming a commercial for Crunch cereal! There is no enemy plot.

"I'll take care of our smart student, officers," Betsy says. "Sorry you were inconvenienced."

They leave and Betsy hands you a sheet of paper and a stack of books.

The paper says:

CAREER COUNSELING TEST ON
METEOROLOGY AND SPACE
1. Define the following cloud formations: a) cumulo-nimbus b) cirrus c) nimbo-stratus d) noctilucent e) nacreous

The other nine questions are just as bad.

Your career in television seems to be a bit clouded.

THE END

"What now?" you ask Agent Larena.

"My chief has help on the way."

"But you blew up the transmitter," you protest. "Does anyone know we're here?"

"Oh, yes," she replies. "As well as stopping their transmission of classified material, the explosion alerted my superiors. We knew Hobart was going to take over a television station somewhere—we just didn't know which one."

"How long will it take to get back on the air?" you ask, thinking about a comedy show you always watch on Saturday night.

"There's an auxiliary transmitter down here," Agent Larena tells you. "They'll be back on the air in about ten minutes. You see, this studio was built for protection against enemy attack."

"Wow!" you say. "What an exciting, glamorous business!"

A loud groan goes up behind you from the assembled staff.

You turn around, surprised.

"It's also a lot of hard work," says Real Larena. "You don't just go to your job every day and collect your money every two weeks . . ."

It's your turn to groan.

You look at her very carefully.

Could she possibly be Mrs. Downing in disguise?

THE END

Actions speak louder than words, you think. *You must do something.*

No one has noticed you enter the studio, and you have already decided on your plan of action. Disabling the cameras and microphones is your only hope. Your eye scans the studio for a master switch.

On the far wall, behind the set, you spy the electrical panel. You flatten yourself against the wall and creep toward it. The bright lights trained on the set make it impossible for Hobart to see the perimeter of the room, and the attention of the cameramen is focused on Hobart and the general.

Your hand is within inches of the switch when you realize that one of the cameras is now focused on you. Then you realize it's NOT A CAMERA! The laser gun is silent. It makes no sound to interrupt the general as he gives out his classified information.

Forget action.

Next time, better try words.

THE END

As you lean over to take the tray of precious jade that Paschal is handing you, you feel a sharp blow on the back of your head.

Everything goes blank.

When you regain consciousness, you and Paschal are sharing a cell in the local slammer.

"Betsy double-crossed us," Paschal whines.

"Dummy!" you shout. "You should have anticipated something like that!"

"What do you think I am?" Paschal growls. "A mind reader?"

THE END